Save the

All families want to give [...] start in life, but in devel[...] that millions of children g[...] and millions more suffer and die because there is no one to treat them when they get sick.

Save the Children is helping in two ways – with clinics and feeding schemes for children who need care now, and with long-term programmes to help communities provide better conditions for their children to grow up in. Often it is something we take for granted – like an immunisation campaign or a clean water supply. Training for local health workers means that mothers have someone to turn to for treatment and advice, while setting up a village vegetable garden brings better food for all the family.

When disaster strikes, whether it's famine, flood, earthquake or hurricane, SCF is ready with immediate help. Many thousands of young famine victims in Ethiopia and Sudan owe their lives to Save the Children's feeding centres and to its fleet of lorries which carried vital supplies through to the areas worst hit by drought. And SCF teams don't leave once the emergency is over, they stay on to help people rebuild their lives.

It's not only families overseas who need Save the Children; SCF has over 100 projects in the UK. Work in this country is concentrated in the inner cities, where many children get off to an unfair start in life as they suffer the effects of poverty, high unemployment and poor housing. SCF runs family centres, youth projects, playgroups for handicapped children and special schemes for the under-fives. Here, as everywhere it operates, SCF's job isn't just to save children, but to give them a life worth living.

Save the Children Fund • 17 Grove Lane • London SE5 8RD

Jokes written by children of the Ladybird Book Club

Design, illustrations and calligraphy by
JUDITH WOOD and MICHAEL NICHOLLS of
Hurlston Design Ltd

Ladybird Books

British Library Cataloguing in Publication Data

You must be joking!—(Hobbies)
   1. Wit and humour, Juvenile 2. English wit and humour
   I. Wood, Judith II. Ladybird Book Club III. Series
828'.91402'0809282   PZ8.7

   ISBN 0-7214-0966-0

Published by Ladybird Books Ltd Loughborough Leicestershire UK
Ladybird Books Inc Auburn Maine 04210 USA

Printed in England

Foreword by
HRH The Princess Royal
President of
Save the Children

Everyone enjoys a good laugh and the members of the Ladybird Book Club eagerly accepted an invitation to contribute to this book and share their favourite jokes with other children. I am sure that another reason for their enthusiastic response was that they knew all royalties from the book would be going to help some of the world's neediest children. Children who still manage to play and laugh in spite of growing up in conditions lacking many of the necessities of life we take for granted, such as clean water, sufficient food and basic health care.

Thanks to the generosity of Ladybird and the participation of children at schools across the UK, this book will generate not only laughter, but also much needed funds to help Save the Children continue its vital work.

Anne

What did the astronauts find in their frying pans?
Unidentified frying objects

First boy: What has eyes but no nose, a tongue but no teeth and is a foot long?
Second boy: A shoe.
First boy: Bless you!

Why don't polar bears eat penguins?
Because they can't get the wrappers off!

How do you start a bear race?
Ready, Teddy, Go!

Where's the spade?

How do you stop a mole digging up the garden? Hide the spade

Why did the boy wake up in the morning to find Concorde in his bedroom? Because he left the landing light on.

A man was looking under the bonnet of his broken-down car. Another driver stopped to help. 'Can I give you a hand?' he asked.
The man replied, 'I'd rather have a tow.'

Where do sick wasps go when they are ill? To the waspital

There were three identical witches and no one could tell which witch was which.

How do you make a band stand? Hide all the chairs.

Where do frogs hang their coats?
In a croak room

What made the farmer cross? Somebody walked on his corn.

What has feathers, wings and fangs?
Count Duckula

What goes at 125 miles per hour and is yellow?
A train driver's egg sandwich

Jon: Were you invited to Jim's party?
Ron: Yes, but I can't go.
Jon: Why not?
Ron: The invitation says six to eight and I'm nine.

Why do bees have sticky hair?
Because they always use honey combs.

There was a man walking down the street with a cabbage on a lead. Another man came along and said, 'Why have you got that cabbage on a lead?'
'Cabbage? The man in the pet shop told me it was a collie.'

Which airline do fleas fly on?
British Hair Ways

Why is the letter 'T' like an island?
Because it's in the middle of water.

Why do birds in a nest always agree? Because they don't want to fall out.

Where do astronauts leave their space ships? On parking meteorites

Who wrote Oliver Twist?
How the Dickens should I know?

Why did the nurse tiptoe to the cupboard? So she did not wake the sleeping pills.

What did the digital clock say
to the alarm clock?
Look! No hands!

Why is a football pitch wet?
Because the players are always
dribbling.

What do feet eat for breakfast?
Corn flakes.

How do you
know a sausage doesn't
like being fried?
Because it spits.

What's
round and green
and goes camping?
A boy sprout

Two little ants were racing as
fast as they could across the top
of a box. 'Hey!' puffed one ant.
'What are we running so fast
for?'
'Can't you read?' said the other.
'It says right here, tear along the
dotted line.'

What do you get if you cross
a zebra with a pig?
Striped sausages

What did the
chicken say when its
mother laid an
orange? `Look
what mar-mar-laid.'

First eskimo: Here we are, home at last.
Second eskimo: Thank you for letting me stay in your igloo.
First eskimo: Oh that's all right, just put your things in the corner.

Have your eyes
ever been
checked?
No, they've
always been
blue.

What did the robot say to the
petrol pump? Take your finger
out of your ear when
I'm talking to you.

Did you hear about the fight in
the biscuit tin?
The bandit hit the yoyo with a
club, tied him in a blue ribbon
and got away in a taxi.

Knock! Knock!
Who's there?
Howard
Howard who?
Howard I know?

3

Knock! Knock!
Who's there?
Egbert
Egbert who?
Egbert no bacon.

Knock! Knock! Who's there?
I don't know. I haven't
answered the door yet.

KNOCK! KNOCK!

Do you know me?
Yes.
Will you know me tomorrow?
Yes.
Will you know me next week?
Yes.
Will you know me next month?
Yes.
Will you know me next year?
Yes.
Knock! Knock!
Who's there?
Don't tell me you've forgotten
me already!

Knock! Knock!
Who's there?
Godfrey
Godfrey who?
Godfrey hairs
on my
chest.

Knock! Knock!
Who's there?
Amos
Amos who?
Amosquito just bit me.

Knock! Knock!
Who's there?
Cows go
Cows go who?
Cows go moo not who.

Knock! Knock!
Who's there?
Andy
Andy who?
Andy just bit me again.

Knock! Knock!
Who's there?
Luxembourg
Luxembourg who?
Luxembourg just done one on the window.

Knock! Knock!
Who's there?
Luke
Luke who?
Luke through the keyhole and find out.

Knock! Knock!
Who's there?
Tanya
Tanya who?
Tanya tum and help me.

Knock! Knock!
Who's there?
Europe
Europe who?
Europe early this morning.

Knock! Knock!
Who's there?
Tennis
Tennis who?
Tennis five plus five.

5 + 5 = 10

Knock! Knock!
Who's there?
Irish stew
Irish stew, who?
Irish stew in the
name of the law.

Knock! Knock!
Who's there?
Felix
Felix who?
If he licks my
lolly once more,
I'll thump him!

Knock! Knock!
Who's there?
Granny
Granny who?
Knock! Knock!
Who's there?
Granny
Granny who?
Knock! Knock!
Who's there?
Aunt
Aunt who?
Aunt you glad that Granny's
gone?

Knock! Knock!
Who's there?
Ivor
Ivor who?
Ivor let me in or I'll climb
in the window.

Knock! Knock!
Who's there?
Adolf
Adolf who?
Adolf ball hid me ind de moud
and I cand dalk proder.

CROSS THE ROAD JOKES

Why did the hedgehog cross the road?
To see his flat mate.

Why did the orange cross the road?
To play squash.

Why did the cock cross the road?
To show his girlfriend that he wasn't a chicken.

Why did the chicken cross the football pitch?
Because the referee shouted, 'Foul!'

When is it bad luck to be followed by a black cat?
When you're a mouse

What did the egg mayonnaise say to the fridge?
Close the door, I'm dressing.

What did the orange juice say to the water?
I'm diluted to see you.

Why was the theatre crying?
Because the seats were all in tiers.

What is green and goes up and down? A gooseberry in a lift

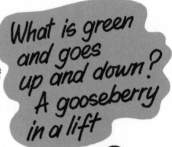

Who looks after sick gnomes?
The National 'Elf' Service

I used to tap dance until I fell in the sink.

What do you do if you want to join Dracula's fan club?
Send your name, address and blood group on the back of an envelope.

What is a ring leader?
The first person to use the bath.

What lies in a pram and wobbles?
A jelly baby

What do you feed parrots on?
Polyfilla

Beware of the Cat

Why did the teacher go to the optician? Because he had bad pupils.

Teacher: If you had 10p in your pocket and you asked your dad for another 10p, how much would you have?
Boy: 10p, sir.
Teacher: You don't know your arithmetic, boy!
Boy: No sir, you don't know my dad!

What goes 100 miles an hour underground?
A mole on a motorbike.

What do you call a teacher with earplugs?
Anything, she can't hear you!

Teacher: How many feet are there in a yard?
Boy: It depends on how many people are in the yard.

Teacher: What does it mean when the barometer falls?
Boy: Er.... the nail has come out of the wall, sir?

Boy: I think my teacher loves me.
Girl: Why do you say that?
Boy: She puts lots of kisses in my books.

$5 \times 6 = 27\frac{1}{2}$ X
$8 + 3 = 14$ X

Why did the boy take a car to school? To drive the teacher up the wall.

What do you get if you cross
a cow, sheep and a goat?
A Milky Bar Kid

What made the
postage stamp?
It saw the letter box.

Why don't millipedes play
football?
*By the time they've tied on their
boots, the game is over.*

What do
hippies do?
Hold your
leggies on.

What do
young hurricanes
do for amusement?
Play draughts.

Why do bears have fur coats?
*Because they would look silly in
anoraks.*

What do spacemen play
on their way to the moon?
Astronauts and crosses

Where do sheep get
their hair cut?
The baa baas

Who is green and has wrinkles?
The Incredible Hulk's granny

The judge said
to the dentist,
'Take out the tooth,
the whole tooth
and nothing
but the tooth.'

What's round and furry and
smells of mint?
A polo bear

Who ate his victims two by two?
Noah Shark

Look
Both
Ways

What's grey, has a trunk and four legs?
A mouse going on holiday.

What is the difference between lightning and electricity?
You don't have to pay for lightning.

What is 300 feet high and wobbles?
The Trifle Tower

What do you get when you cross a giraffe with a hedgehog?
An eleven metre hair brush

What ballet is most popular with monsters?
Swamp Lake

What's green and big and sits in the corner?
The Incredible Sulk

What's brown and furry and has a trunk?
A mouse coming back from holiday.

What was Noah's profession?
An Ark-i-tect

If there are two tomatoes on a plate, which is the cowboy?
Neither, they are both redskins.

Who invented fire?
Some bright spark

What do you do if you can't find the M6?
Drive up the M3 twice.

What do you give a sick bird?
Tweetment

Doctor! Doctor!

Doctor Bell fell down the well,
And broke his collarbone.
A doctor should attend the sick,
And leave the well alone.

Doctor! Doctor!
I feel like a pack of cards.
Wait over there and I'll
deal with you later.

Doctor! Doctor! I keep feeling
like a sheep.
That's baaaaaad!

Doctor! Doctor! I feel
like a cricket ball.
How's that!

Doctor! Doctor! I feel like a bridge.
What's come over you?
Two buses, three lorries, two cars...

Doctor! Doctor!
I feel like a spoon.
Well, sit in the surgery and don't stir.

What do vampire doctors say?
Necks please!

Doctor! Doctor! I can't get to sleep!
Lie on the edge of the bed and you'll soon drop off.

Patient: Doctor, I've swallowed a bone!
Doctor: Are you choking?
Patient: No, I'm serious.

Doctor! Doctor! I feel like a pair of curtains.
Pull yourself together, lad.

Where do cows go for their holidays? Moo York

What did the hat say to the scarf?
You hang around while I go on a head.

Where would you find a prehistoric cow? In a moo-seum

How do you make an apple puff? Chase it round the garden.

What is wrapped in cling film and lives in bell towers?
The lunchpack of Notre Dame

What is green and bounces up and down? Spring cabbage

What goes through the water at 100 miles an hour? A motor pike

Who was the first underwater spy?
James Pond

What bird never sings?
A ladybird

Why do giraffes have long necks?
Because they've got smelly feet.

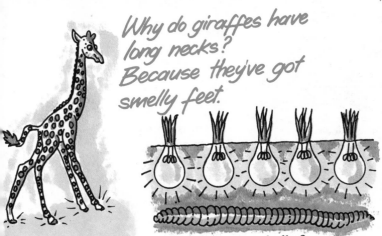

Why do we plant bulbs?
So worms can see where they are going.

What did the policeman say to his stomach? You're under a vest.

What do you get if you cross Dracula with snow?
Frost bite

What exams do farmers take?
Hoe and Hay-levels

A man is in a cell. There is a table and chair in the room but there is no window or door. How does he get out?
He chops the table in half. Two halves make a whole. He crawls through the hole and he is out!

What man is round, and lies in the road?
A manhole

Why did the farmer roll his field of potatoes?
Because he wanted mashed potatoes.

Stereo for Sale

Hooray!

Three pieces of string went into a pub. The first one went up to the barman and asked for a pint of beer.
'Are you a piece of string?' asked the barman.
'Yes.'
'Get out, we don't serve string.'
The second piece of string went up to the bar and asked for a pint of beer. He was sent out too.
The third piece of string went up to the bar.
'Are you a piece of string?' asked the barman.
'No, I'm afraid not.'
(A frayed knot)

What did the stamp say to the letter? Stick with me, baby.

What's green with red spots? A frog with measles

What did the pink panther say when he trod on an ant?
'Ded ant, ded ant, ded ant, ded ant, ded ant!'

What is white and green and jumps up and down? A frog sandwich

What do you call a train loaded with toffee?
A chew chew train

What do you call two thieves?
A pair of nickers

What do you call a cowboy with paper trousers?
A rustler

What do you call a robot when it has fallen in a puddle?
Metal Mucky

What do you call two rows of cabbages?
A dual cabbageway

What do you call a Spaniard who has just come out of hospital?
Man well

What do you call a girl with a tile on her head?
Ruth

What do you call a man with a spade on his head?
Doug

What do you call a man without a spade on his head?
Douglas

What do you call a man who's been buried under the ground for 70 years? *Pete*

What do you call a sleeping bull?
A bulldozer

What do you call a robbery in Peking?
A Chinese take-away

Will the man who had the spotty trunks on, come to the paying office to collect them.

What do you get when you cross a witch with a icecube?
A cold spell

What's the difference between a fish and a piano?

You can't tuna fish.

What is yellow and very dangerous?
Shark infested custard

What does Rabbit want to do when he grows up?
He wants to join the Royal Hare Force.

Why are goldfish red?
Because the water makes them rusty.

Help!

Noah was in the Ark looking out to sea and his wife stood at his side. She saw a hand in the sea and said to Noah, 'What is that in the sea?'
Noah said, 'Oh never mind that, it's only a little wave.'

What has a broom and lives on the beach?
A sand-witch

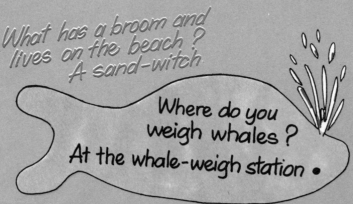

Where do you weigh whales?
At the whale-weigh station.

What's big, grey and wobbles at the knees? A jellyphant

Why do elephants paint their toe nails red? So they can hide in cherry trees.

What do you get if a herd of elephants tramples over Batman and Robin?
Flatman and Ribbon

What do you get if you cross an elephant with a pool?
Swimming trunks

What's the difference between an elephant and a mouse?
An elephant makes bigger holes in the skirting board.

How do you know when there's an elephant in bed with you?
He's the one with the letter E on his pyjamas.

What do you take from a witch to make her itch?
Answer: W

Why did the orange roll down the hill?
Because it had run out of juice.

Do you see any change in me?
No.
Well, I just swallowed a five-pence piece.

Where do frogs borrow money?
From a river bank.

What do you get if you cross a sheep, a kangaroo and pot of glue?
A woolly jumper.
But what about the glue?
I thought you'd get stuck on that one.

Why did the boy bury his radio?
Because the batteries were dead.

What do you call an alligator on wheels?
A rallygator

Why did the secretary put a clock under her desk?
She wanted to work overtime.

Why don't cats shave?
Because 9 out of 10 viewers said they preferred whiskers!

How do you make varnish vanish?
Take the r out.

What is a horse's favourite game?
Stable tennis

Limericks

There was a young man from Dungall
Who was invited to a fancy dress ball.
He said he would risk it
And he went as a biscuit.
But a dog ate him up in the hall.

There was a young man called Jim
Who thought he would go for a swim.
He felt such a fool
When he jumped in the pool
Because there was
no water in.

Humpty Dumpty sat on a wall.
Humpty Dumpty had a great fall.
All the king's horses and all the king's men
said, 'Scrambled egg for dinner again!'

A man stood on a bridge one night,
His lips were all aquiver.
He gave a cough,
His leg fell off and floated
down the river.

There was an old man
from Leeds
Who swallowed a packet
of seeds.
A great big geranium
grew out of his cranium,
And his eyebrows were
covered in weeds.

BLACK
&
WHITE

What is
black and white, black and white,
black and white ?
A penguin rolling down a hill

What's black and white,
black and white and red all over ?
A blushing zebra

What did the first penguin say to the next penguin?
Last one in the pool's a chocolate biscuit.

Why was the Egyptian girl worried?
Because her daddy was a mummy.

What is a beetroot?
A potato with high blood pressure

What's the difference between a hungry mouse and a mouse that's just finished its dinner? One mouseful

What is the height of nonsense?
Two bald men fighting over a comb.

What goes snap, crackle and pop?
I'll tell you next week – it's a cereal (serial).

What do frogs drink?
Croak-a-cola

Why is New York's sky cleaner than London's?
Because they've got more skyscrapers.

What did the beaver say to the tree?
It's been nice gnawing you.

Where is a cat's favourite place to go on holiday?
The Canary Islands

Why didn't the sheep dog pass his driving test?
Because he couldn't make a ewe turn.

Skeleton Jokes

Why did the skeleton run up the tree? Because a dog was after his bones.

Why do skeletons hate winter? *Because the cold goes right through them.*

What do you get if you leave bones out in the sun? A skeletan

Why could the skeleton not go to the ball? *Because he had no-body to go with.*

GHOST JOKES

What did the mummy ghost say to the baby ghost?
Spook when you're spooken to

What did one ghost say to another?
Do you believe in people?

What's a ghost's favourite dessert?
Ice scream

What job did the lady ghost have on an aeroplane?
An air ghostess

How does an octopus go into battle?
Well armed

Car owner: Have you managed to start my car?
Mechanic: No, your battery is flat.
Car owner: Oh dear, what shape should it be?

How do you make a snooker table laugh?
Tickle it with a cue.

There were two men working on a building site when a bear came and joined in the job. When their teabreak was up the bear went back to find his pick, but it was missing. The foreman said, 'Didn't you know? Today's the day the teddy bears have their picks nicked.'

Angry man: I'll teach you to throw stones at my greenhouse.
Boy: I wish you would. I've had ten shots, and I still keep missing!

Mum: Kathryn, what will you do when you get to be as big as me?

Girl: Diet!

There's a man at the door dressed like Long John Silver. *Tell him to hop it.*

Boyfriend: Mr Smith, I've come to ask for your daughter's hand in marriage.
Father: Sorry son, you've got to take all of her or nothing!

The ants and the earwigs were having a football match. The ants were winning by one goal to nil. At the end of the first half the manager of the earwigs told Jo, 'Get your boots on, you're playing.' By full time Jo had scored ten goals and all the crowd shouted, 'Earwig Jo! Earwig Jo! Earwig Jo!'

Mother: Who's that at the door?
Son: A woman with a pram.
Dad: Tell her to push off!

What did the table-cloth say to the table? Hands up, I've got you covered.

What happens if you play tennis with a rotten egg?
First it goes ping and then it goes pong.

What happened to the cat who swallowed a ball of wool?
She had mittens.

What do you call a boomerang that never comes back? A stick

What animal is an illustrated book?
A cat-alogue

Do Robots have brothers?
No, only transistors

How do you spell hungry horse with only four letters? M.T.G.G.

What's purple and has sixty legs and big teeth?
I've no idea, but if you meet one, run.

Why is the letter 'A' like a flower? Because a 'B' always comes after it.

They have invented a new rocket made completely out of wood – wooden nose cone, wooden cockpit.
Trouble is – wooden go!

Three slightly deaf grannies were walking down the street.
The first granny said, 'Windy isn't it?'
The second granny said, 'No, it's Thursday.'
The third granny said, 'I'm thirsty too, let's go and have a cup of tea.'

What advice did Dr Dracula, the psychiatrist, give his patient? 'Fangs' for the memory.

What's the difference between a
dog and a flea?
*A dog can have fleas, but a flea
can't have dogs.*

What is small, white and laughs a lot?
A tickled onion

Why did the Romans build
straight roads?
*Because they did not want to
drive their horses round the
bend.*

How do worms fall over? With great difficulty

What's the meaning
of minimum?
A very small mother

When do astronauts have
their dinner?
At launch time

Why did the strawberry cry?
Because his mother was in a jam.

What sits in a bowl and shouts for help?
A damson in distress

What's yellow and stupid?
Thick custard

How do you cut a sea in half?
With a see (sea) saw

How do you get a baby astronaut to sleep?
Rocket

What do you call a
snake on a car?
A windscreen
viper

What do you call a woman who balances a pint of beer on her head, a pint of beer on her elbow and plays snooker at the same time?
Beatrix Potter

What do you call three lemonade bottles? A pop group

The Fizz

What do you call the man who comes in through your letter box?
Bill

What do you call a lady who burns her bills?
Bernadette

JUNGLE JOKES

Why are there no aspirins in the jungle?
Because the parrots eat 'em all (paracetamol).

How do you cook sausages in the jungle?
You put them under a gorilla.

What's a crocodile's favourite game?
Snap

Where do baby apes sleep?
In apricots

Why is it dangerous to play cards in the jungle?
Because there are too many cheetahs about.

Why do birds fly south
for the winter?
It's too far to walk.

What do porcupines eat with
cheese?
Prickled onions

Customer:
Do you have a book
called
"How to become a
millionaire"?
Bookshop assistant:
Who is the author?
Customer:
Robin Banks

The Earthquake by Major Disaster

Football by QP Ranger

Crowds at the Seaside by Que Upa

Breakfast is Ready by Cris P Bacon

The Haunted House by Hugo First

Chinese Golf by Holin Won

The Broken Window by E Z E Didit

Where does Donald Duck come from?
Out of a quacker

How do you count cows?
With a cowculator

How does an eskimo build his house?
Igloos it together.

Why did Robin Hood steal from the rich? Because the poor had no money.

Try and Try Again by Percy Vere

The Party by Sir Prize

Don't Fall by Eileen Dover

Only me by I Malone

My automobile by Iona Karr

Walking Across the Road by J Walker

Dial Again by Ron Number

Electrical Faults by Lou Swires

Ladybird would like to thank the following schools for their help in making this book possible:

Amblecote Primary School, Stourbridge

Arborfield, Newland and Barkham
C of E Junior School, Reading

Bloxham C of E School, Bloxham, Oxon

Brennand's Endowed Primary School
Clitheroe, Lancs

Broadfield East First School, Crawley

Carnalridge Primary School, Portrush
Co Antrim, Northern Ireland

Cedars First School, Harrow Weald
Middlesex

Chuckery Junior School, Walsall

Constable Primary School, Hull

Contin Primary School, Strathpeffer
Ross-shire

Cross-in-Hand C of E Primary School
Heathfield, East Essex

Cross Primary, Ness, Isle of Lewis

Dale St County Infants School
Ulverston, Lancs

Denholme First School, Bradford, W Yorks

East Deane Junior and Infant School
Rotherham

Ellel St John's C of E Primary School
Lancaster

Elton C P School, Bury, Lancs

Fulneck Boys School (Junior Department)
Pudsey, West Yorkshire

Grafton C of E (Controlled)
Primary School, Marlborough

Griffithstown Infants School
Pontypool, Gwent

Guiting Power Primary School
Cheltenham, Glos

Heighington Primary School
Newton Aycliffe, Co Durham

Highfield Grove Middle School, Stafford

Hockering V C School, Norwich

Holland Park C P School, Clacton-on-Sea

Hollyhedge Junior and Infant School
West Bromwich

Hythe C of E Primary School, Hythe, Kent

Kendall C of E Primary School, Colchester

Killylea C P School, Co Antrim
Northern Ireland

Little Bollington C of E (Controlled)
Primary School, Altrincham, Cheshire

Littleton First School, Evesham

Marshland Middle School, Doncaster

Martley C of E Primary School
Martley, Worcs

Mary Towerton First School
High Wycombe

Monkwick Infants School, Colchester

Mosspits Lane Infants School, Liverpool

Mountfield Junior School
Newcastle Upon Tyne